A farmer had a donkey to carry sacks of corn to the mill. The donkey was getting old. He had been carrying the heavy sacks for a long time, and he was looking thin and tired.

One morning, the poor old donkey heard the farmer muttering about a plan to get rid of him.

"There are bad times for me ahead," said the donkey to himself.

So that evening, the donkey escaped from the farm and set off on the road to Bremen.

"When I get to Bremen, I shall sing songs in the street to earn some scraps for my dinner," he said to himself.

The donkey was happy with his plan. He trotted along the road, until he spotted a dog. The dog looked lost and sad.

"What is the matter?" said the donkey.

"I am old and frail, and I can no longer hunt," sniffed the dog. "So I have been chased out from my home."

“That is terrible,” said the donkey. “But you must not get upset. You can come to Bremen with me, and sing songs in the street.”

So the donkey and the dog trotted off happily along the road, until they came to a lonely cat.

"Good evening, Kitty," said the dog politely. "Why are you looking so sad?"

"I got too old to catch a mouse, so my mistress left me by the roadside," said the cat.

“Come with us,” said the dog. “We are going to Bremen to sing songs in the street.”

The cat didn’t need long to think.

“That sounds like fun,” she said. “I will come, thank you.”

So the three animals trotted along the road to Bremen, until they came across a rooster who looked very sorry for himself indeed.

"What's up, Rooster?" said the cat.

"I heard that I am going to be roasted for lunch in the morning!" wailed the rooster.

The cat was horrified. "No, you are not! You will come with us to Bremen instead," she said.

The rooster had no wish to argue with the cat, so the four animals set off. Before long, they became sleepy and started to look for somewhere to rest. They came across a little house. It was well lit. The animals looked in to see three robbers emptying sacks of gold onto the floor.

"What can we do?" said the dog.

"We will drive the robbers out," said the donkey. "Jump on my back, and sing as loudly as you can."

So the dog jumped on the donkey's back, and the cat jumped on the dog's back, and the rooster jumped on the cat's back, and everyone sang loudly.

The animals stormed into the house, still singing, and the terrified robbers fled in panic.

“Argh! A monster!” they cried.

The animals looked around at the empty house. It was snug, and they were all very sleepy so they flopped down on a rug by the fire and went to sleep.

Later that evening, the robbers came back.

“Monsters do not exist,” said one robber to the rest. “We will go and get that gold back.”

As the robbers crept into the house, the door scraped against the kitchen floor. The noise woke the animals.

In an instant, the cat ran at the robbers and scratched them. The dog bit the robbers' legs. The donkey kicked them, and the rooster cried, "Cock-a-doodle-doo!" at the top of his lungs.

The robbers fled again, but for good this time. As for the four animals, they no longer wished to go to Bremen. Instead, they lived happily in the little house for ever more.